How the Moon Regained Her Shape

By Janet Ruth Heller   Illustrated by Ben Hodson

I would like to dedicate
this book to my parents,
Bill Heller
(may his memory be a blessing)
and Joan Heller, and to
Charlotte Dillon and Marilyn Terrill. — JRH

To my mom, and to all those
who look up at the moon and dream. — BH

Thanks to Wesley R. Swift, Jr.,
Observatory Director of the Von Braun
Astronomical Society for reviewing the
"For Creative Minds" section
and verifying its accuracy.

Once the moon was round and full, proud of her gentle light.
She did not fear the darkness around her. She danced across the sky,
laughing as she twirled her skirts.

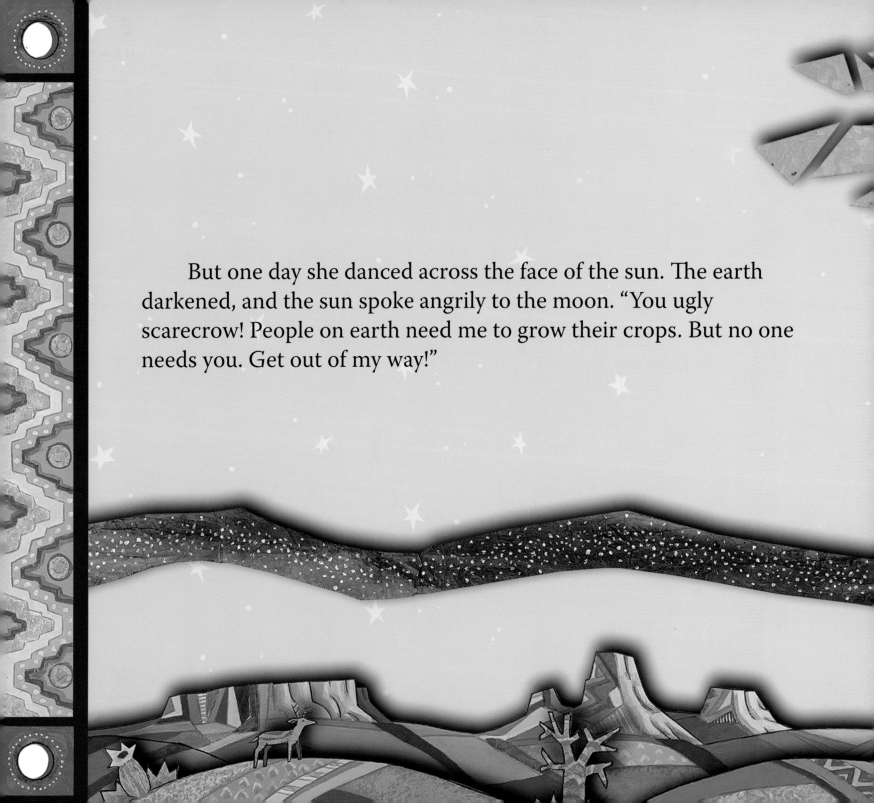

But one day she danced across the face of the sun. The earth darkened, and the sun spoke angrily to the moon. "You ugly scarecrow! People on earth need me to grow their crops. But no one needs you. Get out of my way!"

The moon stopped dancing and blushed very red. "I'm sorry," she stammered. She slowly drifted away from the sun.

The moon tried to start dancing again, but the sun's words tormented her. Her arms and legs seemed too heavy to twirl. She felt very alone in the heavens. She slowly walked along her skypath, hanging her head. Her body began to shrink until she was just a sliver of her former self.

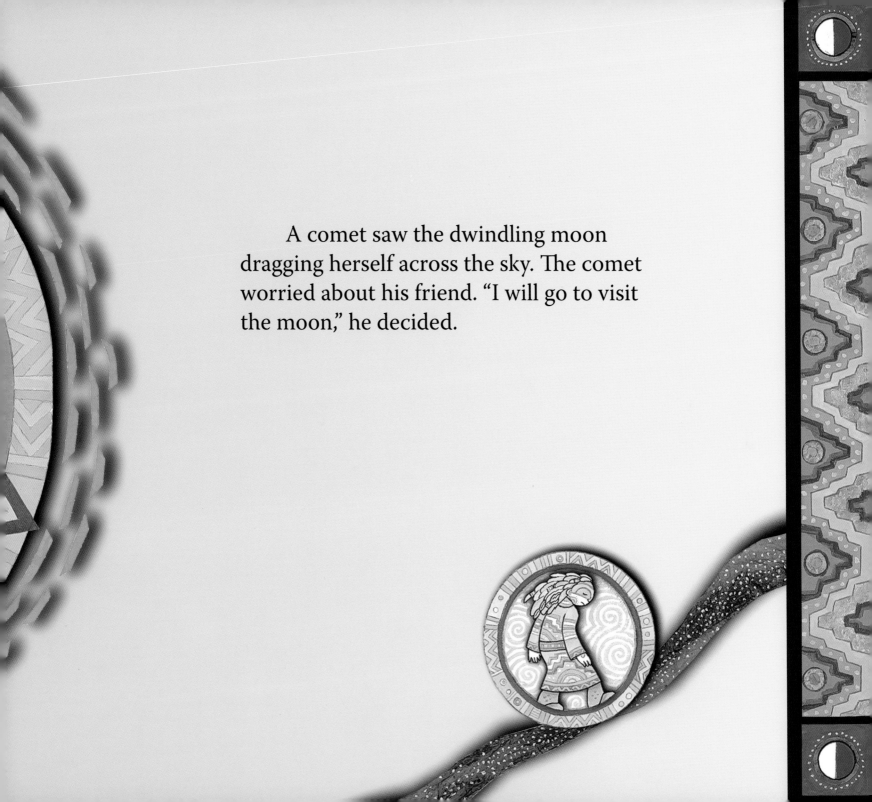

A comet saw the dwindling moon dragging herself across the sky. The comet worried about his friend. "I will go to visit the moon," he decided.

When the comet found out why the moon had gotten smaller, he told his friend, "There is a woman on earth named Round Arms who can restore you to health. She lives at the foot of a mountain." The comet gave the moon directions to the woman's home.

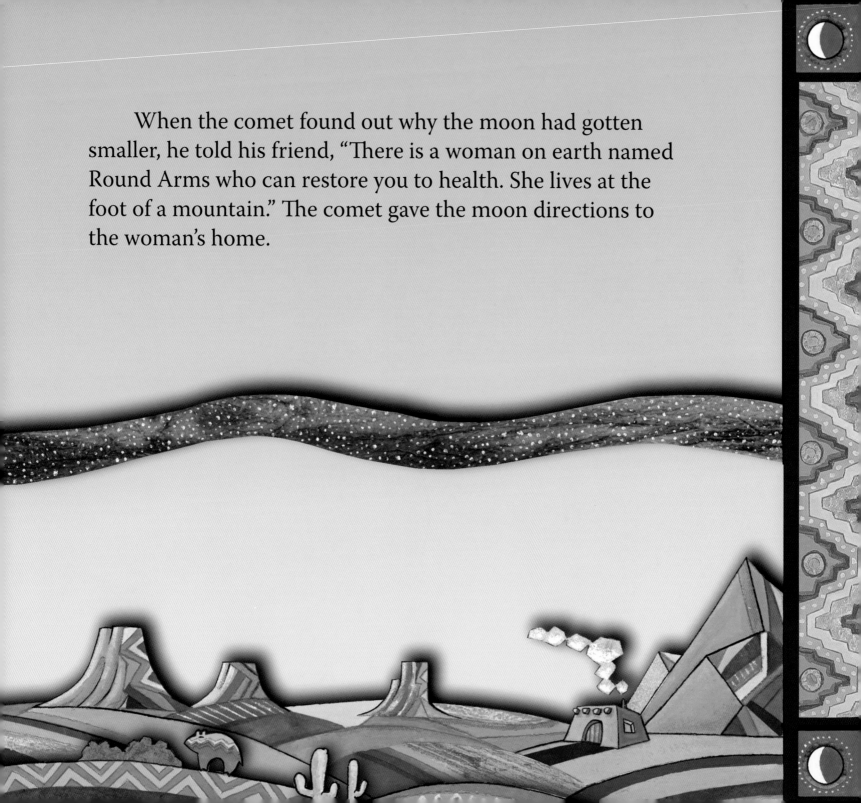

The moon trudged to the mountain where Round Arms lived. By the time she reached Round Arms, the moon was nearly invisible.

Round Arms came to the door of her hut to greet the moon.

She was a big woman with long, dark braids and bronze skin. Her brown eyes gleamed. "Welcome, Sister Moon. You look cold and tired. Come into my home for some tea."

The tea tasted like mint and ginger, and the moon felt refreshed. She told Round Arms about the sun's taunt.

Round Arms gently hugged the moon and dried her tears. "The sun has a bad temper and sometimes speaks cruel words. Hold my hand, and I will take you where you can hear what those who love you are saying."

Round Arms led the moon to the home of Painted Deer, the artist. Painted Deer was drawing a picture of a forest at night.

"I miss the moon," he said. "The light of the moon makes the forest dreamlike and beautiful, and that is what I want to paint." The moon smiled and began to hold up her head.

Then Round Arms took the moon to a rabbit hole.
A mother rabbit was feeding her two bunnies.

"I wish the moon would come back," the mother whispered. "In her moonbeams we can romp safely and find the corn and sunflowers that Painted Deer has left for us." The moon laughed and grew larger.

Then Round Arms took the moon to a
field where a hundred women danced and sang.

We sing to the moon, our sister,
Who pulls the seas to the sands,
Who changes her shape like a magician,
Who lights our paths at night.
Return to the sky, our sister,
For we miss your gentle beams
And your loving smile.

Round Arms and the moon joined the women's dance.

After the dance ended, the women gave the moon a beaded necklace, and the moon gave them tiny bells in return.

Her eyes sparkling with joy, Round Arms hugged the moon again. "I will return to the sky, Round Arms. I will never forget what I have learned. The sun has his job and his admirers, and I have my job and my friends."

The moon danced and sang all the way back to her skypath. Now, whenever someone insults her and she dwindles, she remembers her good friends on earth. Then the moon regains her strength and fullness.

For Creative Minds

Moon Observations

The months as we know them (January, February, etc.) are **solar**, based on how many days it takes the earth to revolve around the sun, roughly divided by twelve. A **moon-th**, or **lunar** (moon) month, is based on how long it takes the moon to orbit around the earth.

The **phases** (shapes) of the moon change according to its cycle as it rotates around the earth, and the position of the moon with respect to the rising or setting sun. This cycle lasts about 29 ½ days.

A **lunar** (moon) month starts on "day one" with a **new moon**. The sun and the moon are in the same position and rise and set together. We can't see the new moon.

The moon rises and sets roughly 50 minutes later each day.

The moon appears to "grow" or it **waxes** each day from a new moon to a full moon. The waxing moon's bright side points at the **setting sun** and can be seen in the late afternoon on a clear day.

A **crescent** moon is between new and half (less than half full), and may be waxing or waning.

The **half-moon waxing** or **first quarter moon** occurs about a week after the new moon. The moon is a quarter of the way through its rotation, but it looks "half full." The first quarter moon is highest in the sky when the sun sets.

A **gibbous** (fat) moon is between half and full (more than half) and may be waxing or waning.

As it approaches full, the moon appears to be getting bigger and is visible in the east in the afternoon. About two weeks after the new moon, the **full moon** rises when the sun sets and sets when the sun rises. The full moon reaches its highest point in the sky at midnight.

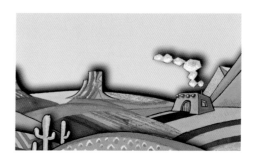

New Moon

Waxing Crescent

First Quarter

Waxing Gibbous

Full Moon

The moon appears to get smaller, or to **wane**, after the full moon. The bright side of the moon points to the **rising sun**.

The **half-moon waning** is also called the **third-quarter moon** because it is three-quarters of the way in its rotation around the earth. The third-quarter moon is highest in the sky when the sun rises and can be seen in the morning on a clear day.

As the moon approaches its new moon phase once again, its sliver (or crescent) is visible in the eastern sky just before sunrise, then after the new moon, in the western sky just after sunset.

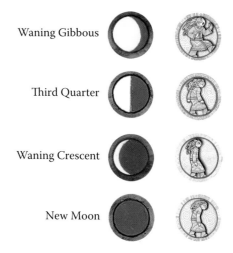

Waning Gibbous

Third Quarter

Waning Crescent

New Moon

A Lunar Project

Look up the moon-rise in your newspaper, in an almanac, or on the Internet. Mark the new moon as "day one" on a calendar. Each day, keep your eyes open to see whether you see the moon. Draw a picture of what it looks like on your calendar. Do this for one full lunar month.

What is a "blue moon?"

The phrase "once in a blue moon" means something that happens occasionally or not very often. A **blue moon** happens when there are two full moons in one calendar month. For example you might have a full moon on the 1st or 2nd of a given month and then another one on the 30th or the 31st. The second full moon is the blue moon.

Learn More

To learn more about the phases of the moon and view these graphics, go to the *How the Moon Regained Her Shape* home page at **www. SylvanDellPublishing.com**.

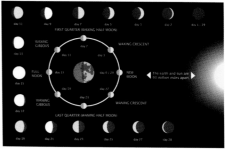

238,855 miles (mean)

diameter: 7,926 miles

diameter: 2,160 miles

Native Americans kept track of the seasons by naming each of the full moons. Different tribes had different names based on their lifestyles or surroundings. *See if you can figure out why the tribes used these names and which part of the country these tribes might have lived in. Check out some of the links for the answers.*

January	February	March	April
Wolf Moon Old Moon	Snow Moon Hunger Moon Opening Buds Moon	Worm Moon Crow Moon Crust Moon Maple Sugar Moon	Grass Moon Planter's Moon Fish Moon
May	**June**	**July**	**August**
Flower Moon Budding Moon Corn Planting Moon	Strawberry Moon Rose Moon	Buck Moon Thunder Moon Sturgeon Moon Green Corn Moon	Fruit Moon Barley Moon
September	**October**	**November**	**December**
Sap Moon Harvest Moon	Harvest Moon Hunter's Moon Falling Leaves Moon	Frost Moon Beaver Moon	Long Nights Moon Cold Moon

How to Deal with Bullies

In this story, the sun bullies the moon. A bully is someone who hurts other people either physically or verbally. Sometimes the bully acts this way to get something or to feel important. Usually bullies feel bad about themselves, and they act out their angry feelings on others.

If someone bullies you, you may need the help and support of your friends, just as the moon does in this story. Here are some ideas to help you deal with a bully:

- Try to avoid the situation or place where you are being bullied, or try to avoid being alone.
- Don't show anger or fear; that is exactly what the bully wants. Try to keep a neutral expression, to laugh, or to make a joke if you can.
- Ask the person to leave you alone and then walk away.
- Talk about the problem with your best friends. Maybe they have some ideas for you. For example, a friend might tell you that the kid who annoys you also mistreats other people. Or your friend might tell you how he or she handles the bully.
- It is very important that you talk to your mother, father, grandparent, teacher, principal, or the school's counselor about the problem, especially if someone in your class frequently hurts your feelings, threatens you, or physically attacks you. Nobody deserves to be treated badly by others. It is not tattling to talk to an adult about a bully.
- Consider taking a class in self-defense. There are many classes for young people in karate, judo, or other martial arts. Such training can give you self-confidence and teach you how to block blows and frustrate attackers.
- A group of kids may help you to stand up against bullies and to find a way to prevent bullies from hurting anyone else.
- Remember that one person's insults or punches do not make *you* a bad person. Think about your friends and family members who like and care about you. If someone bullies you, tell other people about it until someone helps you.

Thanks to Laura Goldberg, PhD, Child Psychologist, Newburyport, MA for her help with this section.

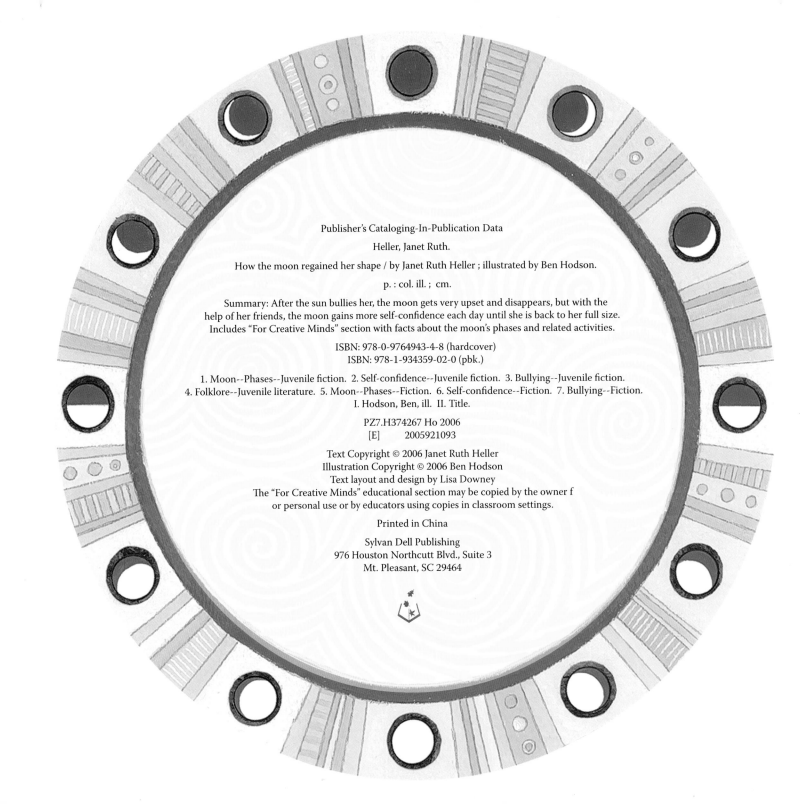

Publisher's Cataloging-In-Publication Data

Heller, Janet Ruth.

How the moon regained her shape / by Janet Ruth Heller ; illustrated by Ben Hodson.

p. : col. ill. ; cm.

Summary: After the sun bullies her, the moon gets very upset and disappears, but with the help of her friends, the moon gains more self-confidence each day until she is back to her full size. Includes "For Creative Minds" section with facts about the moon's phases and related activities.

ISBN: 978-0-9764943-4-8 (hardcover)
ISBN: 978-1-934359-02-0 (pbk.)

1. Moon--Phases--Juvenile fiction. 2. Self-confidence--Juvenile fiction. 3. Bullying--Juvenile fiction.
4. Folklore--Juvenile literature. 5. Moon--Phases--Fiction. 6. Self-confidence--Fiction. 7. Bullying--Fiction.
I. Hodson, Ben, ill. II. Title.

PZ7.H374267 Ho 2006
[E]   2005921093

Printed in China

Sylvan Dell Publishing
976 Houston Northcutt Blvd., Suite 3
Mt. Pleasant, SC 29464